The Unicorn

Dana Simpson

Andrews McMeel
PUBLISHING®

Complete Your Phoebe and Her Unicorn Collection

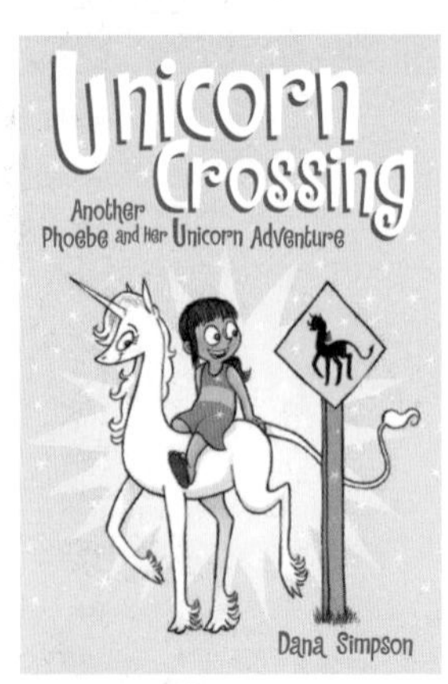

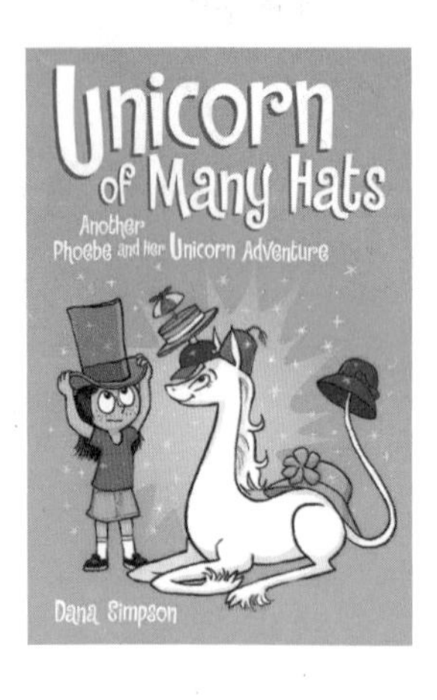

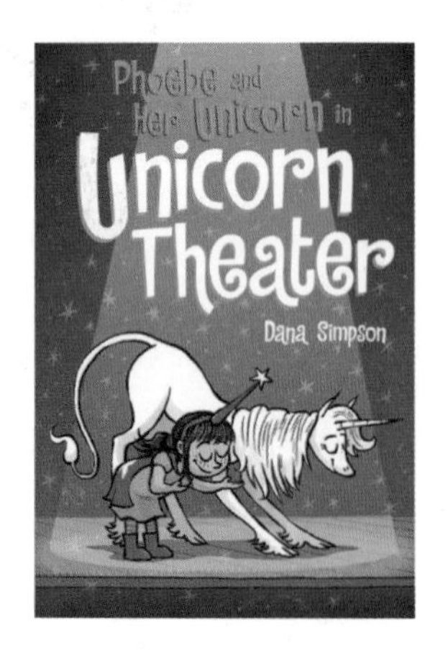

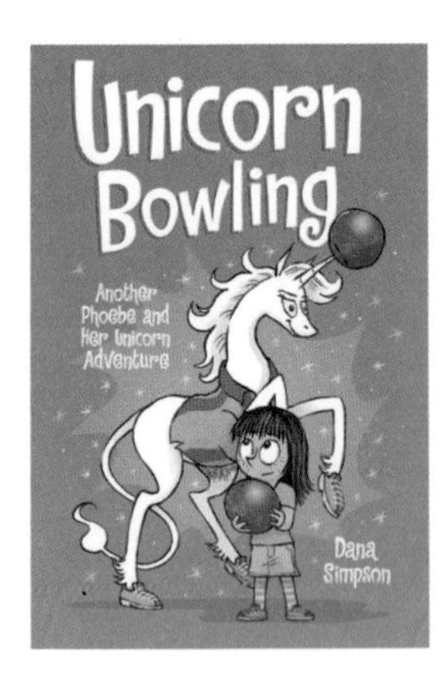

Hey, kids!

Check out the glossary starting on page 172 if you come across words you don't know.

Stargazing makes most people feel LESS significant.

Little green unicorns! A stunning emerald hue.

dana

Knock knock!
Who is there?

Interrupting cow!
Oh, you mean Mabel?

I did not realize you knew Mabel. How has she been?
The joke doesn't work if you know an ACTUAL interrupting cow.
I have not seen her since she inevitably stopped being invited to parties.
dana

Summer's gonna be over soon. I wanna go out with a *BANG!*

What sort of bang?
Let's have a slumber party!
dana

An EXPLODING slumber party?
What? No!

Whew! Then I am in.
Yeah, the bang is totally metaphorical.

Mom, can I have a slumber party?
Sure.

I already invited Marigold. I...want to invite Max, too.

You know, traditionally, girls don't invite boys to their slumber parties.

Traditionally there aren't any *unicorns* at them, either!
Good point. *Viva la revolución.*
dana

Come on in, Max!

So what're we gonna do at this slumber party?

I vote we do nothing but prance around and eat oats!
dana

That seems like more of a "you" thing.
We could prance and eat cereal. Compromise!

Max, I know you like space stuff.
And Marigold, YOU pretty much like anything to do with unicorns.
We ARE the best.
dana

Right. So, I wanted us to watch something we'd ALL be into.
So allow me to present...

That one episode of *Pastel Unicorns* that's set on Neptune!
Best episode.
Indeed.

It's weird, sleeping in someone else's house.

The night sounds are different. That clock...the train horns in the distance...

The snoring unicorn...
Isn't it weird how she snores arpeggios?
Z
dana

I really hope Max had fun at our slumber party.
I am sure he did.

After all...
It included a unicorn.

Max is more into robots.
Oh! Then I should have invited Stephanie.

You know a robot named Stephanie?
Two, in fact! It is quite confusing.

sniff

siiiiiiigh

How long are you going to sit there smelling your new school supplies?
How long until the first day of school?
dana

Look at how the ducks gather around us. They're hoping for some bread.
QUACK?
QUACK?

I notice you did not bring any today.
Nope. I'm not gonna do that anymore.

I read on a nature website that feeding ducks bread is bad for them. No nutritional value. Keeps them from eating stuff that's GOOD for them.

But it's one thing to *KNOW* that...

And a whole other thing to see all those hopeful ducks, and give them NOTHING.
I can't even EXPLAIN it to them. Ducks are too stupid.
QUACK?
dana

You must be strong. For the ducks.
For the ducks.

This is the first time I've ever had to practice TOUGH LOVE.
Ducks are good practice for that.
QUACK.

I'm not ready to go back to school! I want summer to go on forever.
But...I also AM ready, because I've had time to prepare myself. And doing nothing all day has started to get boring.
Do unicorns ever feel two things that seem to contradict each other?
Oh, certainly.
dana
I often feel that BOTH sides of me are my best side.
Someday you'll have a REAL problem, and I'll be there for you.

On the first day of school, it's always really hard to focus.

Could you cast some sort of... *focus spell* on me?
I could...

But I must warn you, a focus spell is difficult to calibrate, so it carries certain risks.

Could you repeat that? I got distracted by that pine-cone.
I shall prepare the spell.
dana

Young lady, class started five minutes ago.
I know. I'm stuck.

You are NOT stuck.
My unicorn cast a concentration spell on me, and now I'm obsessed with that one floor tile.

I'm guessing you don't have a NOTE saying that.
Notes from my unicorn tend not to help much.
dana

YOOOUUU GOT IN TROUBLE, YOOOUUU GOT IN TROUBLE

First day of school, and you already gave me one thing to tease you about.

...aren't you gonna, you know, REACT?

Can't now. Unicorn cast a concentration spell on me.
TWO things.
dana

How did the concentration spell work out for you?

The results were really mixed.

I kept getting stuck concentrating on random things, but I also got a week's worth of home-work done in class, so my afternoons are free for a while.
Also...I think my freckles might be turning rainbow-colored.
A temporary side effect, but a stylish one.
dana

G'night, kiddo!
Wait...

Tell me a story.

Aren't you getting a little old for bedtime stories?

Says the adult who watches more cartoons than I do.
Once upon a time, there was a very observant little girl.
dana

Phoebina. And her parents were the king and queen of a magical far-off land!

King Ethan and Queen Emily were very proud of the princess, whose best friend was a unicorn.

King Ethan and Queen Emily were very proud of Princess Phoebina.
They were her parents. Parents have to be.
It wasn't just that.
She was smart. And weird. And way better than the king at Ultra Go-Kart Racing 8.
He wasn't just letting her win?
That wouldn't have been very kingly of him.
dana

One day, King Ethan took the princess out for ice cream.
Quadruple-scoop ice cream.

We both know that's more than you can ever finish.
We correct in fiction what life gets wrong.
dana

And what do you suppose the king and the princess did next?
dana

They went home.
That's all?

If they had an ACTUAL adventure, I'd never be able to sleep.
You're pretty self-aware for a kid.

Hello, Princess Phoebina.

Oh, hey, um, Double Marigold.
Yes, we wish to speak with you about that.

Why MUST you imagine us double? Is one unicorn insufficient?
dana

I love you so much, I want to MAXIMIZE you.
We are mollified.
Speak for yourself!

pss pss pss

What?
I said, pss pss pss

Speak normally, please.
Fine.

But so much for my career as a "unicorn whisperer."
I like you just fine as a unicorn normal-voice-talker.
dana

Oo, a BUSINESS PERSON!
Where?
Not in real life! I have downloaded a popular unicorn game onto my horn.

It is called POKHÚMON GO.
dana

I THOUGHT you seemed distracted.
Oo, is that a FLIGHT ATTENDANT?

Pokhúmon Go is a big hit with unicorns!

It is a lot of fun.

THOK

It is also highly distracting.
dana

We unicorns got the idea for Pohúmon Go from you humans, of course.

If *YOU* can enjoy pretending to catch magical creatures, we can pretend to capture you back.

Of course, my "Phoebe" remains the jewel of my collection.
Aw, you're sweet. And thanks for not trapping me inside a ball.
dana

Please pass the popcorn!

We have a perfectly good TV in the other room.

Yeah, but it's fun watching movies with a PROJECTOR. It's like going to the theater.

And EVERYONE is okay with this?

It's a talent. She likes showing it off.
So long as Phoebe keeps feeding me popcorn, I am happy as a clam!
dana

Again?
I fear so.

I don't mind saving you from staring at your reflection, but isn't there a better way?

We have not found it, through all the years.
Well, there's only been a PHOEBE for the past nine.
dana

I do not know if I CAN stop being mesmerized by the beauty of my own reflection.

Well, you *ARE* really pretty.
Tragically pretty.

I could help you really see your flaws.
dana
You are such a good friend.

You NEED to be able to look away from your reflection. Focus on your flaws!

Don't you ever think "ew" when you look at, like, your nose hairs?
dana

My nose hairs are lovely, like the bristles on an elegant crystal brush!

I do admire your self-assurance.
My nostrils are...dare I say it... heavenly.

Maybe you wouldn't have to stare at your reflection if you were LESS PRETTY.
dana

What if you made a really weird face every time you saw your reflection?

AAA NOT WORTH IT.
Sometimes the cure is worse than the disease.

Maybe this will help!

I do not like how weird these ornaments make my face look.
Exactly!

EVERY time you see your reflection, just imagine it's THIS reflection, and you'll be able to look away.

What if it just makes me start giggling?
Well, that's fun too.
dana

Aw. After all that, you're STILL stuck staring at your reflection?
I am not stuck. I have CHOSEN to be here.

It is good to be able to ENJOY the things we love, even if it would be bad to be imprisoned by them.
dana

Okay, well, have a good gaze.
Do not go far. I may still need rescuing later.

Do I talk too much? Dakota says I talk too much.

If I talked too much, you'd tell me, right? I'd want to know. Or maybe I wouldn't. I'm not sure. I guess I never really know how I'll react to something until it's happened.

I guess I kind of think on the outside. I'm not sure why it helps to have someone there to hear it, but it totally does.

I talk a lot around Dakota 'cause she makes me nervous. But around YOU it's 'cause I'm totally comfortable. Isn't that funny?

Anyway...DO I talk too much?

I am quite all right with you as you are.
Thanks.

How'd you get to be such a good listener?
I just think about how lovely I am, until you are finished.

Hello, Phoebe!
Hey, Marigold.
PORTABLE HOLE
BOO

What should we do today?
Oh, well...
PORTABLE HOLE
BOO

I really need to sit here and do this history report.

Then I shall regale you with tales of the history of unicorns!
I've already done two about that, and it's a long school year.
dana

Phoebe! Are you done with your history report, yet?
I'm not! We can hang out LATER.
This is important to me. I need to do well to get a good grade this quarter!
Wait. So there are things that matter to you MORE than unicorns?
Apples and oranges.
I refuse to compete with fruit.
dana

Rar.
Oh, hello, Todd.

Rar rar?
No, Phoebe is off doing some sort of history report.

It should not bother me, but I am feeling left out and underappreciated.
dana

Rar rar.
You always know the right thing to say.

Rar rar rar?
No, Phoebe will probably be done with her history report eventually.

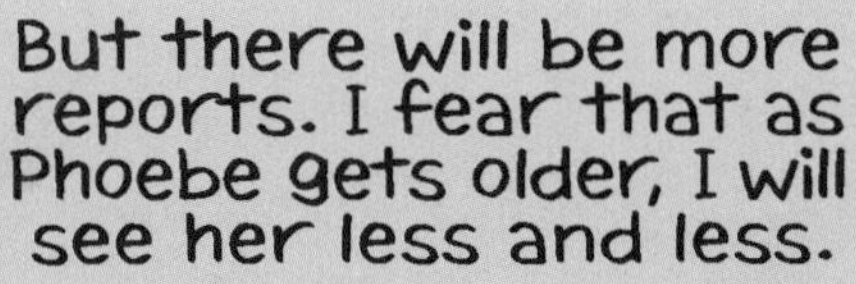
But there will be more reports. I fear that as Phoebe gets older, I will see her less and less.

Rar rar.
Yes... I am still sure she is my best friend.

Rar.
Yes, you ARE lighter to carry, but part of that is that Phoebe wears clothes.
dana

ping
Ah, it is a text from Phoebe! She has finished her history report and is ready to hang out.
Rar rar rar?
No, we can finish our walk. I waited for Phoebe...she can wait for me.
Rar rar.
Yes, you are a good conversationalist too, just in a different way.
dana

Hey!
Phoebe! You are done with your history report!

What is it about?
Georgia Neese Clark, the first female Secretary of the Treasury!

You know, you are probably the first child of EITHER gender to regularly ride a unicorn to school.
dana

Maybe some future kid will write a report about that!
I believe the Shield of Boringness could be relaxed that far.

The harbor's rough today! Check out the whitecaps.

In times of old, we believed those were UNICORNS, trapped in the sea.

As a little filly, I was taught the tide was a UNICORN TRAP, and if I stayed too long on the beach...

...the sea would take me, and I would spend the rest of my days hanging out with fish.

A *terrifying* fate, as fish are known to be poor conversationalists.

Unicorn legends are kind of unfocused.
LIFE is kind of unfocused.
dana

Hey, can I jump rope with you?

Well, see, we WOULD let you play...

...but the new jump rope chant we came up with is ABOUT you, and that's just awkward.

Lemme guess...you rhymed my name with "dweeby" again.
"Squeegee," actually. We're proud of that one.
dana

Stupid Dakota won't jump rope with me.
I am sorry.

I could jump rope with you!
You? Really?

You sound surprised!
Well, you don't have *HANDS*.

Once again, you are being *DIGITIST*.
Once again, that's not a word.
dana

Okay, I brought a jump rope.

ZAP

Cooool.
dana

Will it also recite rhyming chants for us to jump to?
Magic cannot do ALL the work.

Once, long ago, a unicorn named *Chrysanthemum Goldenflanks* was fond of constantly jumping in place, and everyone made fun of her.

Hey, I, um... I wanna jump rope with you and the unicorn.
Welllll...

Okay, but I get to make up the first chant we do.
Nngh. Okay, fine.

DAKOTA, DAKOTA, SHE SMELLS LIKE A GOAT-A
Be kind, Phoebe.
dana

Next time, I DON'T think I'll have you enchant my bubble wand.
dana

I used to ride the school bus
(It was crowded, as a rule)

But that was then, and now I ride
A unicorn to school!

Sometimes I used to miss the bus
My mom would get irate

But now however long I take
My unicorn will wait.

I saw the world through windows
That were high above the ground
YIELD

But now I see and hear and smell
The beauty all around.

I still could ride the school bus
(It's one way to get to school)
BUS STOP

BUS STOP
dana
But take my word that unicorns
Are way way WAY more cool.

That tree has wood nailed to it.

Did someone find the amount of wood on this tree insufficient?
I think it's for climbing.

Oh, I see. Having hands is not enough for tree climbing. Humans must have ALL the advantages.
dana

You sound bitter.
MY only way into a tree is to jump REALLY HIGH.

What do you see up there?
It looks like...
A platform! Like, sort of a tree house!
I want to see! I will get a running start and jump up!
How big a running start do you need?
Not far. Three or four zip codes.
dana

I wonder who put this tree platform up here. It's practically in my backyard.

We could claim it for ourselves!
It could be our CLUBHOUSE.

I shall cast a *spell of befuddlement,* and none shall find it while we are present.

So we're just gonna commit platform theft?
They should not have left it lying around in this tree.
dana

If this is gonna be a clubhouse, we need to become a club!

What sort of club should we found?
Why not a FAN club?

You could fan me whilst I luxuriate and eat grapes.
dana

That isn't how fan clubs work.
It is how the GOOD kind of fan clubs work.

The first order of business in this clubhouse shall be-
BLART!

BLART BLART BLAART!
He says this is HIS tree platform, and we are trespassing.

I thought you cast a befuddlement spell so no one would find us.
BLAART BLART BLART BLAART BLAART BLART
Those do not work on goblins, who are perpetually befuddled.

BLART!!
Now he is complimenting your shoes.

I guess we need our OWN clubhouse.

If we must have one, we shall have the finest!

I shall summon pixies to labor a hundred days and nights on a magical tree fortress such as the world has not seen!
dana

Could we have one sooner than that?
If you are happy with just TWO balconies.

What should we do for Halloween costumes this year?

We could go as NOTHING. I could render us invisible!

How would anyone know to give us candy, then?
They would not, but nor would they notice if we TOOK the candy.

I think hanging out with humans is making you *devious*.
When I said your species had nothing to teach mine, I was *SO WRONG*.
dana

This Halloween, I think I wanna go as a SUPERHERO.
The one you made up?

I didn't just "make up" Claustrophoebea. She's my SECRET HERO IDENTITY.

I'm declaring right now that CANDY ACQUISITION is one of her superpowers.

That is not a very heroic power.
Heroes deserve candy.
dana

I could HELP you to be a superhero for Halloween.

Thanks, but I already have a costume.
Not just a costume...

I could temporarily give you ACTUAL SUPERPOWERS.
dana

Why am I only NOW learning that this is a possibility?
I enjoy our conversations. I did not want you to go off and fight crime.

Ready?
Hang on. I want to savor this.

This is my ORIGIN STORY.

ZZAP
It's maybe the most important moment in a young superhero's-

I wasn't done.
Once I have the spell queued up, it is a bit like trying to hold in a sneeze.
dana

I don't feel any different.
Well, try and use your powers.

How?
Concentrate.

Focus all your energy on your horn. Plant your hooves to keep yourself grounded...use your tail for balance, if necessary.
dana

Ha ha.
Sorry. They do say all advice is autobiographical.

I'm sure I'll learn to use my temporary super-powers eventually.

I bet it's one of those things I won't even realize I'm doing when I do it.

I just hope it happens before Halloween.
dana

Hey, come back.
You will be fine.

So I have actual SUPER-POWERS?
Yes.

COOOOL! Which ones?
I will let you discover for yourself.
dana

The best part of every superhero TV show is when the hero is first getting to know her powers!

How much time DO you spend watching TV with my dad?
The WORST part is crossover episodes.

Marigold, did you make "instant dish-washing" one of my superpowers?
You are most welcome.

Hey Dad. I have SUPER-POWERS now, thanks to Marigold!

Really? What kind?
Well...

So far, I can levitate a couple feet off the ground, and wash dishes by looking at them.
Sometimes bragging has a heavy price.
An important lesson for a young superhero.
dana

I gave you the power of SUPER DISHWASHING so we would have more time together on chore night.

And I gave you minor levitation powers because it makes you lighter and easier to carry around.

You have a third power you have not yet discovered, which will also serve us both.
dana

So this is mostly about YOU.
Unicorn!

Shimmering castle is under attack!
I know how to stop the DARK BEINGS, Princess Pedantia!

I like that new unicorn.
Sgt. Horsey? He's not new.
Pop!
He's not?
He's a revival of a **first generation** Pastel Unicorn.

Toycorp was trying to get boys into *Pastel Unicorns.*
Sgt. Horsey's mechanical wings are from a crossover with *Robots Who Are Totally Also Cars.*

Some people's dads are into football.
I get to have a daughter who shares my interests.

Hey, Phoebe.
Hey, Max. You can tell who I am?

Well, yeah.
I'm CLAUSTROPHOEBEA. Phoebe is my secret identity.

It's almost like a mask that covers five percent of my face isn't a very good disguise.
dana

Yeah, I can still see your freckles.
CURSE YOU, FRECKLES!

Marigold gave me actual superpowers as part of my Halloween costume!
Whoa, cool!

Do you need a sidekick?
Sure, if you're offering!

I asked Marigold, but she doesn't DO "sidekick." For some reason she'd rather be my *arch-nemesis*.

FEAR THE WRATH OF POINTYHEAD.
It's a side of her you don't usually see.

TRICK OR TREAT!
Make with the candy, Todd.

The way he does that, it's like we're baby birds and he's feeding us.

It's much more appetizing than what birds regurgitate.
Yep.
dana

I bet bird Halloween is really gross.
Rar. Rar rar rar.

How much candy did YOU get?
I don't know...

I keep trying to count it, and there keeps being MORE.

You have discovered your third superpower: CANDY MULTIPLICATION.
dana

None of your powers seem classically heroic.
Spoken like a boy who doesn't WANT extra candy.

Hey, Dakota, nice candy haul.
Yep.

I didn't know goblins could magically multiply candy too.

Actually, we're just so adorable, like, every house gave us tons of extra!
dana

BLAART!
Works better when he doesn't do THAT too much.

Usually Halloween is about dressing up as someone else... but you let me actually BE a superhero for the night.

I feel different! I feel powerful! I feel...

Uncomfortably full of candy.
You have consumed it at a truly *heroic* pace.
dana

What're you reading?
It is an ELECTION GUIDE.

Unicorns can vote?
We can in unicorn elections!

Soon shall come the ELECTION FAERIE.
I can't decide if that makes democracy better, or unicorns worse.
dana

What do unicorns vote on?
There are several initiatives.

This one would impose a sparkle tax. This one would relax regulations on horn polish.

And THIS one calls for the pixies in Unicorn City to shut up.

That seems rude.
They have been singing the same song for 138 years.
dana

For Rainbow Sparkle Princess, I am voting for YOU.

I'm not even a unicorn!
No rule says you must be.

And as my dearest friend, you fill MY heart with sparkles and rainbows.
Well, thanks!

You are likely to lose very badly.
Fine, but YOU'RE writing my concession speech.
dana

Marigold Heavenly Nostrils?
Yes! Hello, Election Faerie.

Ready?
Ahem.

Yes, yes, no, yes, no, no, 57, apples, and Phoebe Howell.

What was that?
Unicorn voting!

I wish it would stop raining.

It will stop eventually.
I still don't really understand why you can't use magic to make it stop.

You have never really understood the unicorn code.

Nature must be allowed to follow its own plan, without excessive magical interference.

Earlier, you made it rain salad dressing on the lawn, before you ate some of it.
dana

Grass being delicious is part of nature's plan.
My umbrella still smells like balsalmic vinaigrette.

AH-
CHOO
Whoa... SPARKLES.

Oh dear. It is YOUR turn to have SPARKLE FEVER.
But that's a UNICORN DISEASE.

It has been known to cross over. Much like that horrible plague I caught from YOU last month.

That was a *cold.*
Sneezing WITHOUT a sparkle explosion. It is so...*unnatural.*

Sparkle fever is not serious in a human. You should be better in time to return to school on Monday.

You mean I'm sick, and I don't even get out of SCHOOL?
11-5
dana
dana

I feel cheated.
Well, if it is any comfort...

It might be awkward to hand in an excuse note saying you are too sparkly to come to school.
Are you kidding? That's a LIFELONG DREAM of mine.

Tag!
Excuse me?
You're it.
I know!

I am *it!* This, that and the other! I am ALL of it.
dana

Now you catch me, and I'LL be it!
I will still be it. I was BORN this way.

MOOOOOOOM! DAAAAAAAAAD!
dana

What?
I had a really bad dream!

I dreamed Marigold started sitting on ME and making me carry her to HER school.

Well, don't worry. That won't happen.
I'm not so sure. I mean... KARMA.
SPACE EXPLOSION

Do you have homework?
Uh... no.

Phoebe...
Okay, yes I do.

But I can't put this book down! Reading is almost like homework I assign MYSELF. It's not as if I'm... um...out *STEALING CHANGE FROM THE WISHING FOUNTAIN.*
dana

I'm actually proud that's the worst behavior you can think of.
Curse you! You've stunted my evil imagination.

I'll just tell you straight up: I didn't do my homework.

I tried to, but I couldn't pull myself away from this book. I accept whatever punishment you feel is appropriate.
dana

I'm also going to leave my book here until the end of the day, because otherwise I know I won't be able to avoid reading during class.

If I assigned self-awareness homework, you'd get an A on it.
Hey, *COULD* you? Then I'd be ahead and have time for reading.

I got in trouble for not doing my homework.
What sort of curse did your teacher place on you?

Will you develop some horrible deformity? Or just lose the ability to taste candy?

I get four gold stars on the behavior board instead of five.
Your human schools may be making you SOFT.
dana

You landed on "chance"! Pick a card.

"You have won SECOND PRIZE in a BEAUTY CONTEST. Collect $10."
dana

SECOND? I and my radiant beauty have been CHEATED! I protest in the STRONGEST POSSIBLE TERMS.

I will not be aesthetically judged by someone wearing THAT mustache.
I notice you still accepted his money.

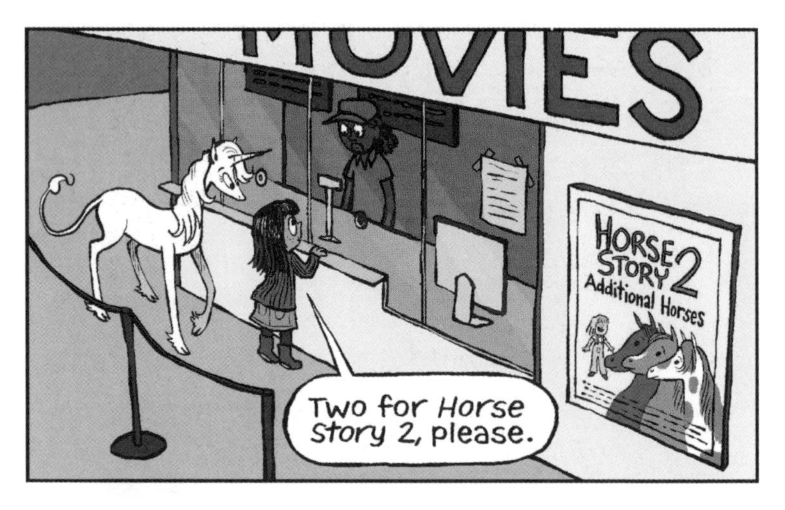
MOVIES
HORSE STORY 2
Additional Horses
Two for *Horse Story* 2, please.

What are you doing?
Turning off my cellphone.

It's theater etiquette, so people can concentrate on the movie.

That is thoughtful of you.

I suppose I should also turn off my majestic glow.
Also thoughtful.

I have a loose tooth! I might lose it soon.
That takes me back to my own fillyhood!
dana
Unicorns get loose teeth too?
Yes, and also loose HORNS.
Unicorns have "baby horns"?
I saved mine! I use it as a toothpick.

A lot of kids believe if you leave your tooth under a pillow, the TOOTH FAIRY will come give you money for it.

But my parents told me that was made up, so I always knew better.

But...the Tooth Fairy is REAL. I KNOW her.
My parents DOUBLE LIED to me about the Tooth Fairy?
I am sorry to have to disillusion you.
dana

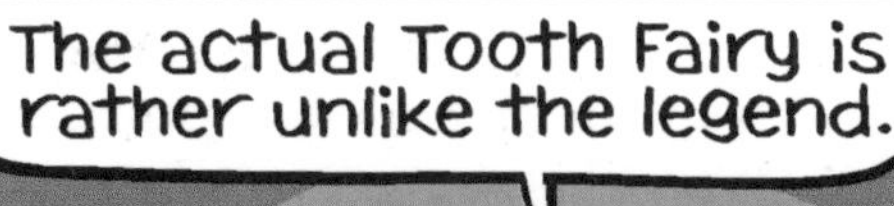
The actual Tooth Fairy is rather unlike the legend.

She does collect teeth, but she is discerning! Her interest is only in unique, special teeth!

She pays handsomely for teeth she finds worthy of the *Tooth Fairy Dental Museum*

Oo, let's go there!
It is small. I would have to shrink us. And the cafeteria is only so-so.
dana

What is up?
I lost that tooth!

And I want to meet the Tooth Fairy, so I'm decorating it to make it INTERESTING enough for her.
dana

What's her favorite color?
Glitter.

Glitter isn't a color.
Try telling Jennifer that!

Marigold! The Tooth Fairy visited.

Did she leave you anything?
Just a note.

"Do not be afraid to leave pieces of yourself behind."

She has paid you with a PEARL of WISDOM.
Someone really needs to teach you magical creatures capitalism.
dana

You have an extra bounce in your step today!
I had a very good dream last night.

I dreamed I was a beautiful, magical creature, whose best friend brought her TWO APPLES.

I only brought you ONE apple.
O woe! Reality is crushingly disappointing.

A shooting star!

We started calling them that before we knew they were meteorites, and we still do even though we know now.

We used to call them UNICORNS WHO HAVE TRIPPED AND FALLEN.

We believed the stars were an invading unicorn army, and when one would slip and tumble from the sky, we would all rush there to interrogate them!
dana

This resulted in MANY unicorns being bonked in the head with meteorites.
OW!

You didn't update your myth?
Well, we had taken repeated blows to the head.

I'm hungry.

BY THE GLORIOUS POWER OF SPARKLES, MAY THERE NOW BE WAFFLES.

dana

I like to retain some ability to surprise you.

Marigoooool d!
...Marigold?

Have you seen Marigold? She's ALWAYS here after school.
Sorry, I haven't.

If she doesn't show up soon, I'll have to take the BUS! I haven't PREPARED for that!

How would you "prepare" for that?
I'd spend every recess smelling the inside of my shoe.
dana

Mom, have you seen Marigold?
No, why?
She didn't meet me after school.
I'm sorry. Would some cocoa help?

Cocoa's good, but it's no UNICORN.
Ah, but these are SPARKLY marshmallows.
dana

MARIGOOOOOLD!

Where is that unicorn?

She probably got stuck staring at her reflection again...I have to find her and save her!

I'll need my INSPIRING HEROIC THEME MUSIC.
DUNNNN DA NAAAAAAAAA

Marigold! THERE you are!
Oh, hello, Phoebe!

I was worried!
I am fine. I have been spending time with this other small human.

Stephanie? That kid who used to, like, idolize me?
Hi, Phoebe!
dana

I've gone from feeling 100% worried to feeling 200% rejected.

knock
knock

Marigold!
I am down to 15% magnificence.

Can I help?
I smell cocoa. The sparkly marshmallows will restore my strength.

What HAPPENED?
I have been overusing my magic.
dana

I can't decide if I'm just concerned for you, or mad because you used up all your magic hanging out with ANOTHER kid.

I cannot use it ALL making your homework disappear.
I didn't ask you to DO that, and I get in trouble when my teacher doesn't believe me.

You used all that magic for Stephanie today? What's so great about her?

It is a MESSAGE ORB. Take it off, please, and it will play.
dana

Hold that thought.

Hello, Marigold Heavenly Nostrils. This is the Unicorn High Council. How are you? We are fine. The poinsettias are especially colorful this year! And we have recently been very into rye toast.

The winter pixies will soon be in season...
Unicorns sure take a while to get to the point.
Ironically enough.

It has come to the attention of the Unicorn High Council that you have EXCEEDED your allotment of magic for this day.

This is just a friendly warning. Have a sparkling day, Marigold Heavenly Nostrils!

You used up MORE magic with Stephanie than you EVER have with me!
dana

In a single day, but you are way ahead, all-time.
That just means she has a higher average score than me.

Give me one good reason you spent all that time and magic on Stephanie instead of me!

She was very sad.
dana

As a unicorn, I was able to give of my time and magic, to make her feel better.

Now I feel guilty.
Normally, I would cast a NON-GUILT SPELL on you, but I am too drained.

I am sorry you felt neglected.
Thanks.

I'm sorry I was jealous.
It is all right.

You are my best friend, and ideally you could spend every moment of your life basking in my boundless wonderfulness.
dana

Even your ego is sweet.
Then it is fortunate it is so much of my personality!

It is the season for magic...so I would like to ask you to grant me a holiday wish.

Me grant YOU a wish?
It is the magic of the season.

I wish for you always to remember that we are best friends, and to know that will not change.

dana
Okay, but now we're even.
Then I will have to ask you to stop drinking from MY cocoa mug.

Look! It's true!

Make a circle on the floor, and your cat will sit in it. The internet was right!

I should go tell the internet that unicorns do it even faster.
Do. The world should know that unicorns will NOT be out-cuted.
dana

We need to get Dakota her shoes back!

This will take our full, combined brain power!

Zap

Or we could do it the easy way.
Unicorn!
BLAART!
dana

I couldn't think of a good New Year's resolution.

I was going to resolve to sparkle less!

But then I worried that would make the world seem dim...so I was going to resolve to sparkle MORE.

But the world does not seem to want for illumination at the moment.

So I will resolve to sparkle EXACTLY the same amount I was otherwise intending to sparkle.

Then I resolve not to change at all either!
You would make a fine unicorn.
dana

Happy new year, Marigold.
Happy years are all well and good, but they can be rather boring.
My finest recent year was when a child hit me in the nose with a rock, resulting in our becoming best friends!
Unhappy new year, then!
CLINK
Thank you, and a rock in the face to you, too!
dana

Phoebe! We have been invited to a goblin opera!
dana

This opera is performed annually, to celebrate the coming of the new year!

In English, its title means something like "The Cycle of the World's Renewal From Beneath the Frost."

In Goblin, it is called *"BLAART BLAAART."*
I really hope my high school offers Goblin as a language option.

Wow...THIS is the goblin opera house?
Sort of.
dana

They rent it from the Pixie Opera Company. Before that, it was always performed inside a large hollow stump.

Seating was limited, the place was crawling with slugs and earwigs, and the refreshments were SORELY lacking.

BLAART BLAAAART
But the ACOUSTICS were breathtak-oh, it is starting!

BLART blart BLAA AART

BLART BLART BLART
BLART

BLAAAART blart blart blart
2017
BLART

The story is hard to follow.
It is more about the poetry of the lyrics.
BLART

This next aria is the centerpiece of the opera. It celebrates the Goddess of Renewal.

dana
Wait, that's-

Dakota?!

I did wonder how we got such excellent seats!
I wanna be in a goblin opera.

Hey, Dakota.
Hey, Phoebe. Wasn't I great?

Why'd you invite us, anyway?
I knew you'd understand that being in a goblin opera makes me COOLER.

My popular, cool friends wouldn't understand that, so I had to turn to you.

If I'm so lame, why do you even care what I think?
We need uncool kids' approval, too. It's called democracy.

Just because it's snowy doesn't mean I can't see you.
Lies! I am camouflaged!
dana

Hey Marigold!
Hello Phoebe!

You smell extra good.
I just took a bath.

What is that?
It's how we humans stay clean.

Oh! You immerse yourself in magic cleansing sparkles too?
Substitute "bubbles" for "sparkles," and yeah, basically.
dana

Basically, a "bath" is where you immerse yourself in warm water and bubbles!

I wish to experience this human tradition.

Lead me to the BATHING CHAMBER!
dana

I'm definitely gonna start calling it that.
Then my bath is already a force for good.

This is the "tub" in which you wash yourself?
Yep.

It is so... *human.*

I expected marble pillars! Fountains! Statues of various winged and berobed beings!
dana

It wouldn't match the rest of our decor.
I will just have to slum it this time.

I see the appeal of this! It is no sparkle shower, but it has its charms.

The bubbles, the warm water...I feel as if I haven't a care in the world.

I believe I am stuck.
I'll go get the Crisco.

We have to do a diorama in class this week. It's a GROUP project.

You do not sound pleased.
I HATE group projects.

I always end up doing all the work, because I'm the only one who cares what grade we get. Then EVERYBODY gets my "A."

Like how other creatures seem more attractive by virtue of standing near me?
...not particularly, no.
dana

PLEEEEEASE PUT ME IN THE SAME GROUP AS MAX...PLEEEEEASE PUT ME IN THE SAME GROUP AS MAX...

Max is the ONLY one here I trust to do his share of a group project.

Maybe if I think "Max" really hard. MAXMAXMAX MAXMAXMAXMAXMAXMAX

Phoebe, Sarah, and Mark.
MAX! I mean darn! I mean...fine.

The other kids in my group project asked me to go to the library during recess to work on it.

Did you go?
Of course not. Why waste my recess?
dana

It's due in two days, so I figure I'll just do the whole thing tomorrow night.

Why not now?
I'm not just working for three, I'm PROCRASTINATING for three.

Missed you again in the library at recess, Phoebe.

Who are you?
I'm Sarah. I'm in your diorama group.

Right. I'll do it tonight.
It's done. Don't worry, we'll put your name on it.
dana

...I don't understand.
Put some glue on your fingers. It'll look like you helped.

I thought I would have to do ALL the work, but this time I didn't get to do ANY of it.

The other kids in the group got me a free B+.

I deserve an F for the amount of work I *DID*, but I deserve an A for the job I WOULD have done.
dana

Perhaps your teacher could average that to a C.
We need to go make a diorama NOW or I'll never be able to move on.

Quick! Everybody get out your communicators!

Look at that. Their "communicators" are five times the size of my phone!

And why does the computer on their ship make all those "beep boop beep" noises? Computers don't make that sound.
dana

Because the actual future is disappointing.
I really wouldn't know.

It wasn't supposed to rain today.

You humans do not control the weather.

Usually we can predict it well enough not to get caught in the rain.

Still, in the end, you are at its mercy.

Perhaps this will teach you humility.

I don't need lessons in humility from YOU.

I can keep this up all day.
Unicorn humor isn't very subtle.
dana

How come you never wear a helmet when you rollerskate?

I am wearing an *INVISIBLE* helmet! It is enchanted so as to let my mane blow freely, but still protect my head.

Unfortunately, they are not available in human sizes, as yet.

They never make the best stuff in human sizes.
Well, I envy your ease in finding fitting pants.
dana

Hey, guess what, Dweeby Phoebe? I got my ears pierced.

Good for you.
So you know how before, I was like maybe THREE times cooler and more mature than you?

This doubles that to like six.

You're making these up as you go along.
Cool people get to have their own math.
dana

Dakota got her ears pierced. She thinks that's yet another way she's cooler than me.

Is she?
Psh. No.

Good, because I would hate to imagine I have been spending so much time with a LESS THAN OPTIMALLY COOL child!
dana

You're being sarcastic.
I am soooo glad you have finally learned to tell.

I don't think I really WANT to get holes punched in my ears just yet.
That is fine.

When I was a young unicorn, horn-piercing was very popular. I considered it myself.

It is actually quite practical. You can use a horn piercing to store a pencil! It is always useful to have a pencil.

You can just put a pencil behind your ear, can't you?
It was a short-lived fad.
dana

On partly cloudy nights like this, when some of the stars are concealed...

...the regular constellations are ruined, but it is an opportunity to invent NEW ones.

That cluster of stars is normally part of the constellation *Steve the Unicorn*, but partly obscured, it looks more like...um...
dana

Cynthia the unicorn?
Yes! Who has much shorter legs than Steve.

That looks fun! May I?
Okay, but I bet it's harder with four legs.
That's cheating.
YOU are free to do it on four legs if you want.
dana

PHOEBE!
Why did you not TELL me?!

Tell you what?
There is a patch of CLOVER in your front yard!

Fill me in! What is the FLAVOR like? Is it RIPE?
dana

I didn't EAT any.
We are VERY different sometimes.

Hey, I found a four-leaf clover!
Oo, you should keep it! It will bring you luck.

But if you should find a FIVE-leaf clover, leave it where it is!

Five-leaf clovers can bring only destruction and DEATH!
dana

I never knew clover had so much power.
Six-leaf clovers are less dangerous, but give me TERRIBLE indigestion.

WHOA!

What is that STRANGE GLOWING OBJECT in the sky? I can't recall EVER seeing it before! It must be a UFO!

We surrender, alien overlords! Just don't HURT us!
dana

Take the girl and the unicorn if you must! Just spare me!
Dad makes this joke on EVERY sunny winter day.

"Xylophone"! 48 points!

"Kqbwyxn."
It is a UNICORN word.
dana

Use it in a sentence.
"'Kqbwyxn,' said the unicorn, as she invented a new word."

MeTub
Hey. If you're watching this, you're THAT much cooler. Welcome to SoDakota.

MeTub
Some viewers have been leaving comments asking about... THESE things.

MeTub
PortableHole37 asks "what's with the little green dudes who keep photobombing?"
BLART

MeTub
Two things. First, they're goblins. I didn't like them at first. I get that they're weird, and they kinda smell, too.

MeTub
But I'm their princess or their Beyoncé or something. Whatever it is, they do what I want and I've decided I like them.

MeTub
BLART
Also, in videos it's called *videobombing*. Get it right, PortableHole37.

Two!
Three!
Four!

Oh, I am very sparkly
but I wish I could
sparkle more!

Oh yes I am very sparkly, baby
But I wish I could sparkle oh so much
more now!

And I would still look good with nine legs
But I have the perfect number,
which is four!

TAKE IT,
PHOEBE!
dana

Good try, but
I still say the
blues isn't your
musical genre.
That makes me
sad. . . .ooh, I could
sing about THAT!

Mom signed me up for swimming lessons.

You know how to swim.
She wants me to learn to swim BETTER.

I wonder if they will teach you the *unicorn stroke.*
I've seen you swim. You basically dog paddle.
A common misconception. Dogs UNICORN paddle.
dana

Well, look who's here to take SWIMMING LESSONS like a BABY.
NO RUNNING IN LOCKER ROOM

You're here TOO.
Yeah, but I'm here for DIVING LESSONS.

I'll be gliding through the air like a dolphin jumping a rainbow, while you're pushing a kickboard back and forth.

Diving ALSO involves a board.
That is SUCH a kickboard thing to say.

Teacher?
Yes, Phoebe?

My frenemy Dakota over there is doing her diving class. Could you assign something that'll REALLY impress her?

It's day one. We start with the basics. Here's your kickboard.

I guess I'll just have to wow her with my OUTSTANDING KICKBOARD TECHNIQUE.
Reach for the stars.
dana

Oh dear...Dakota is watching Phoebe with a derisive smirk.

I must help her! I shall *enchant her kickboard!*

AAAAAAAAAAAAAAAAAAAAAA
dana

Hey, Dweeby Phoebe.
Hey, um... North Dakota.
dana

You're bad at nicknames. But you're weirdly good at swimming.
I never saw anybody with a kickboard move that fast.

Thanks! And that was a really unique dive you did out there.

That was me falling off the diving board when you started zooming around.
Well, I enjoyed it.

Dear Phoebe
Although you are a primate
And are small and strange and pink
On feet instead of hooves you walk
(They sometimes kind of stink)
You still remain my dearest friend
Our love does brightly shine
So please be my platonic
Interspecies Valentine!
Love, Marigold Heavenly Nostrils

Well? Will you?
I might have some issues with your phrasing, but you know I will.
dana

I appreciate your wanting to help...
You are most welcome!

But maybe you should ASK before you cast magic spells that directly affect me.
dana

If I abided by THAT rule, you would not have been surprised yesterday morning by your singing cereal and dancing toast.

Permanent exception for singing food, but ask me about anything else.
Noted.

"But I recently visited Concertina Lovelyflank's Sugar Boutique."

"And there I beheld the most remarkable of unicorn confections:"

"A SUGAR DODECAHEDRON.
Twelve sides of pure sugary goodness."

You know what else has twelve sides? TWO CUBES.
Yes, but that is less fun to say.
dana

AUGHPTHB!
dana

What is wrong?
I WALKED INTO A SPIDERWEB!

So you are feeling pangs of guilt for having destroyed the spider's hard work?
YES ACTUALLY BUT IT'S NOT MY MAIN CONCERN!

Why do spiders bother you so much?
I dunno...it's creepy how they have eight legs!

As a little filly, I knew a UNICORN who had eight legs! Her name was Annabelle.

Although...now that I think about it, Anna and Belle MAY have been two separate unicorns who frequently stood next to each other.
dana

It is funny realizing one still carries childhood misconceptions.
I forget what I was freaked out by, so thanks I guess.

Is dad mowing the lawn?
Yep.
dana

Didn't he mow the lawn like three days ago?
That was *before.*

It's uneven now, and that was really bugging him.
I wouldn't have to do this if you would just eat the lawn more evenly.
You also would not have to if you would just plant some carrots.

You look sad.
This often happens by the end of winter...
dana

I have UNICORN SEASONAL AFFECTIVE DISORDER.

I think my mom has that.
Mine is more sparkly.

My mom takes vitamin D for her seasonal affective disorder.
Unicorns have our own remedies.

We have people throw us awards ceremonies!
dana

scribble scribble

I hereby present you with the Phoebe's Sparkliest Friend Award!
It does not have a gold seal, but I will still frame it.

Dad, I need a raise in my allowance.
Why?
dana

Inflation.

Inflation doesn't happen fast enough to affect your allowance.
Marigold keeps wanting me to buy and blow up balloons for her to wear.
She will not let me cast a helium-exhaling spell on her.

Hey, look, it's PA-HO-EEB! Hey, Pa-ho-eeb.

It's PHOEBE.
Whatever. It's a lame name. YOU'RE lame.

Hey, Marigold.
Hello, Phoebe.

Take me somewhere comforting.
To the pixie-run burger joint!
dana

Human cities are lovely at night.
dana

I often do not think much of them by day, but at night they transform into a sea of glorious lights.

They shine like a million...
Unicorns?

I was going to say glow sticks.
Were not.

Explain.

I can't actually BE a unicorn, but with this novelty prop, I can achieve a rough approximation of your most defining feature.

dana

It is a rough approximation.

MORE TO EXPLORE! A special section featuring words to learn!

GLOSSARY

aesthetically (es-thet-ick-lee): pg. 93 – adverb / in a way that is visually appealing and provides enjoyment and satisfaction through beauty

arpeggio (arr-pej-ee-oh): pg. 11 – noun / the notes of a chord played in order, either ascending up the scale, or descending back down the scale

befuddlement (bee-fudd-uhl-ment): pg. 58 – noun / confusion

berobed (bi-row-bd): pg. 130 – adjective / wearing a robe

capitalism (kah-pi-tuh-lizm): pg. 100 – noun / an economic system in which trade and commerce are controlled by private owners for profit

compromise (kom-pro-mize): pg. 9 – noun / an agreement when two sides "meet in the middle" by giving up some demands in order to still get something that they both want

constellation (kon-stuh-lay-shun): pg. 144 – noun / a cluster of stars that can be linked together to form an imaginary outline or picture (such as the Big Dipper)

extraterrestrial (ek-struh-tuh-res-tree-ul): pg. 5 – adjective / something that is from beyond the Earth and outside its atmosphere

indigestion (in-duh-jest-shun): pg. 147 – noun / the feeling of an upset stomach or discomfort in the upper abdomen, usually caused by diet

karma (car-muh): pg. 89 – noun / the belief that your actions help cause what you experience in the future, or the idea that "what goes around, comes around"

levitate (lev-i-tayt): pg. 70 – verb / to float several feet above the ground

luxuriate (lucks-shur-ee-ayt): pg. 59 – verb / to relax in fancy surroundings, or by consuming fine food and drink

metaphorical (me-tuh-for-i-kuhl): pg. 7 – adjective / relating to a figure of speech in which words are used to make a comparison between two things that are different but have something in common

meteorites (mee-tee-or-ites): pg. 102 – noun / a solid piece of debris from a comet, asteroid, or meteoroid that travels through outer space and the atmosphere to reach the surface of a planet or moon

mollified (mol-lih-fyd): pg. 26 – verb (past participle) / soothed or made calm after being angry

platonic (pluh-ton-ick): pg. 158 – adjective / an affectionate relationship that is friendly in nature rather than romantic

primate (pry-mayt): pg. 158 – noun / an order of mammal including monkeys, apes, and humans

procrastinating (pro-krass-ti-nate-ing): pg. 134 – verb / delaying or putting off until a later time what could be done today

subtle (suh-tuhl): pg. 139 – adjective / understated, muted, or low-key

whitecaps (whyt-kaps): pg. 46 – noun / the part of small waves that form a white foamy top (or "crest") in windy or stormy conditions

Phoebe and Her Unicorn is distributed internationally by Andrews McMeel Syndication.

Andrews McMeel Publishing
a division of Andrews McMeel Universal
1130 Walnut Street, Kansas City, Missouri 64106

www.andrewsmcmeel.com

19 20 21 22 23 SDB 10 9 8 7 6 5 4 3 2 1

ISBN: 978-1-5248-5196-5

Library of Congress Control Number: 2019932740

Made by:
Shenzhen Donnelley Printing Company Ltd.
Address and location of manufacturer:
No. 47, Wuhe Nan Road, Bantian Ind. Zone,
Shenzhen China, 518129
1st Printing—7/15/19

Look for these books!

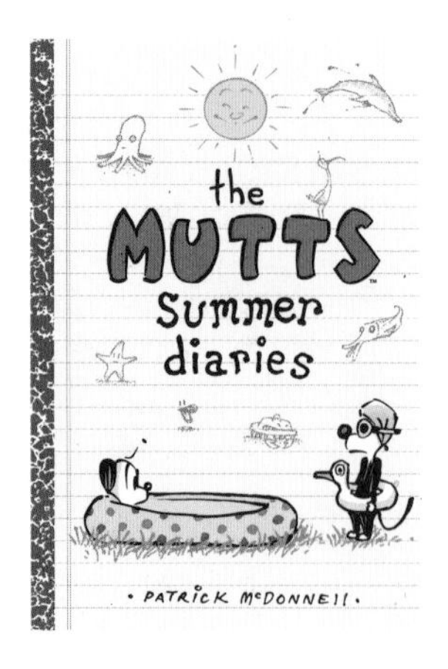

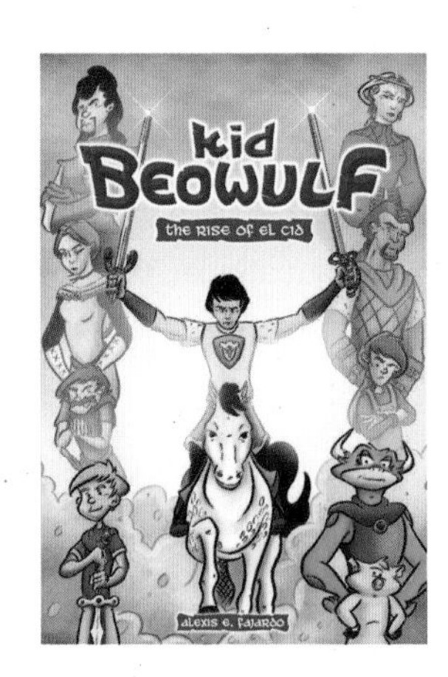